Albert Blows a Fuse

Tom Bower

A LION PICTURE STORY
Oxford · Batavia · Sydney

Meet Albert. He doesn't ask for much. All he wants is a quiet, ordinary life. Ask him what he most likes to do and he'll say, "gardening".

He likes listening to the radio too. Take Tuesday afternoons, for example. Albert would never miss "Teddy Timpson's Toe Tapping Teatime Tunes". It was the radio show he loved the most, and one afternoon they were playing his special song...

when suddenly the radio went dead. Albert knew what was wrong—it needed a new fuse. He looked everywhere for one—in the cupboard, behind the clock, under the cat—but he couldn't find a fuse anywhere.

So he went to "David's Repair Shop" in the High Street.
"David's Repair Shop" is one of those places that sell everything —
plugs, wires, tools, nuts, bolts—

everything, that is, except fuses.

"Tell you what," said David, "Why don't you try that new shop, 'Noyze', in town?"

So Albert did.

"Fuses?" said the owner. "Don't make me laugh! There's no money in fuses. How about a lovely new TV instead?"

"But I only came in for a..." stammered Albert, his eyes wandering around the dazzling shop.

The shop owner showed Albert the television sets—how to turn up the volume and brightness. It was mind-boggling—but fun!

"Perhaps you'd like a satellite dish and a video as well, sir?"
"Next time!" joked Albert. He thought that they looked ridiculous and laughed at the very idea of actually buying one. Albert paid for the television and staggered out of the shop with it.

It was rather tricky getting the television home. And it was even trickier making it work. It was worth all the trouble, though, because when the TV eventually burst into life it was wonderful!

The soaps! The sport! The films! The advertisements! The advertisements? They were as good as the shows—if not better. Albert realized that there was a whole world out there absolutely bursting with things to buy. There was no time to lose!

Albert began to realize that he was missing a lot of good entertainment on the other channels—so he bought a video. But he still had to leave the television to prepare his meals. So he got a microwave. He also moved his fridge and bed into the new TV room so he would never have to move— except to go to the loo, of course.

Soon, Albert had no money: this was not surprising because he had spent it all at "Noyze". He decided to sell his beautiful garden to Mr and Mrs Green next door.

But he didn't mind—he could now buy more things. He particularly wanted a satellite dish.

"Wonderful, this technology," Albert muttered to himself as he phoned "Noyze" to order four new televisions, an extra video machine and a satellite dish or two.

Albert stacked up all his equipment in his TV room. He could watch thirty different pictures at the same time. It was a bit noisy, and the television sets did stop the sun coming in. Albert didn't care though—he could see the pictures better without any sunshine.

"Boring old sun! Boring old people! Boring old world!"
said Albert, switching channels on his remote control.

One morning, some months later, Albert woke to find a bird sitting on the end of his bed. The bird was holding some flowers in its beak. Albert was just about to chase the bird out of the room when he noticed how beautiful it was. Its feathers were smooth and shiny and its eyes were as black as night. Albert took the flowers from the bird. They reminded him of his garden.

Then something unusual happened: the bird hopped around and pecked at all the controls with its beak. The TVs went dead and the videos stopped whirring. There was silence. The peace was wonderful.

Albert felt sad when he remembered the lovely garden. How silly he'd been! There was a beautiful world out there—and it hadn't been made for him to sit inside in the gloom all day.

Albert rushed out of the back door—and flattened his nose
on the fence. He'd forgotten that he had sold the garden.
Albert sat on the step with his head in his hands.

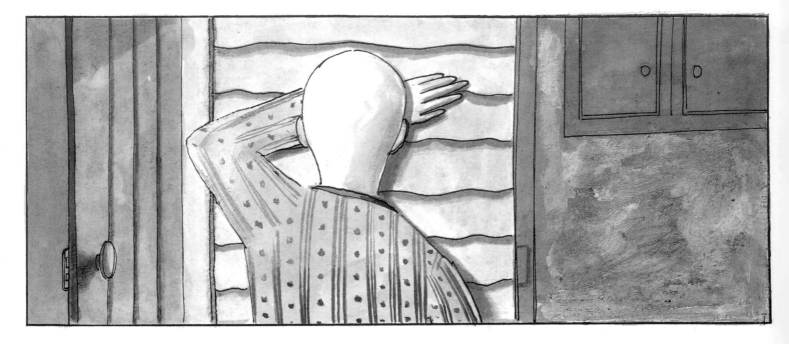

"Hello," said a small voice. "What are you doing out here? Is
your television broken?" It was Mr and Mrs Green's lad, Peter.
    Peter's mum came out to see what was going on. Albert
looked so miserable that Mrs Green couldn't help feeling sorry
for him.

"Would you like your garden back, Albert? It's far too big for us anyway."
Before Albert could answer, Mrs Green leapt into action and yanked at the fence. She puffed... and panted... and pushed and pulled...

"You have a go, Albert!" she gasped. It wasn't that easy—weeks of sitting in front of the TV had taken its toll on Albert's muscles. Mrs Green didn't mind, though—she just kept on pushing!

Nowadays, Albert and the Green family share one big garden. It's fun working together—and it's also quite useful: Peter does the bits that Albert can't reach, and Albert does the bits that Peter can't reach.

Albert still doesn't know what made all the TVs go dead—but he's glad that they did. Life with the Green family is great—real people are much more fun than TV.

And the television sets?
They were useful after all!